Fundamental Matter

Unforsaken Ancient Chinese Tales

Ralph K Jones

RALPH ✉ jONES

Table of Contents

Is This a Game?

Is This a Game?

A cool breeze blew through the forest. The trees rustling made an eerie echo throughout the area. Mai stirred. She felt the cold seep up from the ground, and a sense of uneasiness flowed through her. She opened her eyes, slowly at first. All the while, she struggled to make sense of where she was. No such wisdom was to be had. Only a dark forest greeted her, barely lit by pale moonlight from above.

"Where am I?" Mai asked herself in a desperate need for things to start making sense. "Am I in the game? It's so real?!"

Mai had volunteered to be a beta tester for a new game. She had driven out to the coast and signed a pile of paperwork. But she didn't remember what happened next. Mai knew it was supposed to be cutting edge VR, but this was so far beyond what she expected. She looked like herself. She felt like herself.

"This is weird," Mai said, her calm coming back over her. "But if this is a game, I can win it...I win every game."

She struggled to get up, but her arms seemed unwilling—or at least, unable to help. She stopped to assess the problem and realised that her hands were bound behind her back with tight rope. She struggled to free her hands, but found the rope to be unyielding. She rolled over, struggling to sit up using her body and her legs. She shook her brown wavy hair out of her face and took a look around. She appeared to be in a clearing, sitting in a bed of orange and yellow leaves at the base of towering trees. She was dressed for the outdoors, with a thick, blue cotton coat over a black and violet dress. She wore dark grey leggings and black boots on her feet. Mai knew that if she had any hope of winning the game, she had to find some way to get her hands untied and to get her feet under her again. It was a game like any other—face a challenge and move onto the next. She shimmied until she was on her knees, and then carefully rocked back until her feet were flat to the ground. As carefully as she could, she straightened her legs while raising herself up and maintaining her balance. Though she was now on her feet and at a higher perspective, there was not much more to be seen. She was still in the moonlit dark and still utterly alone.

She nodded to herself, decided that if she succumbed to doubt, she would not make it very far. She began walking, careful to keep her footing lest she fell without the use of her hands to help her. The moon was casting a significant light from above, but the trees casted long shadows that she couldn't see through. The graphics of the game were terrific...was she even *in* a game or was this all happening in her mind? Visions of beasts and monsters hiding in the impenetrable darks danced in her head. She admitted that even though she knew it was only a game, she feared them, nonetheless. She looked around for something that could be used cut the ropes on her hands. The low light made that a nearly impossible search.

Mai continued to walk. Time passed, she knew, but how long she had no real way to gauge. She began to wonder how close the morning might be, desperately thinking about what the warm light of the sun might do to her decidedly dire situation. She was shaken from her pondering as her feet sank into the earth. She flailed around, fighting to keep her balance and not fall face first into the soft terrain. Though she managed to stay standing, her feet refused to move any further. As hard as she tugged on either foot it would not budge, the telltale suction schlep of mud holding her booted feet securely in place was heard as she tried to move. She wished desperately to be able to use her hands, realising that her biggest chance of escape was to undo her boots and step out of them.

"This just keeps getting worse," Mai commented with a sigh. "What's next?"

A low growling came from the shadows to answer her question. It chilled Mai to her bones. She had been so preoccupied with the challenge of getting her hands untied that she hadn't been trying to be stealthy. She had trudged around as if she was wearing a bell and had attracted the worst possible attention.

Mai scanned around, not able to spot the wolf, but it's presence was unmistakable. She struggled again with her feet, but it became clear that as long as the laces were done up there would be no easy way to escape them. She weighed her options and they weren't good. Her hands were tied. Her feet were trapped. And she had absolutely no way to defend herself from the attack when it came.

The Wrong Target

The Wrong Target

The feeling of motion in space is relative. There was inertia, but without landmarks and other things to push past the ship, it was hard to tell the difference between drifting and faster than lightspeeds. However, as the ship's engines kicked in, a rumble could be felt through the entire ship. Commander knew then that it was moving—and moving fast.

"We have a gravitational marker on the ship we are rendezvousing with," Samson said proudly. "We will be there shortly. Not only can we pinpoint them mid-jump, but we can also move about four times faster than they are. We will be on them in record time."

"We hold several records with this ship already," one of the ops officers explained. "All unofficial of course. We cannot really take credit for them until the ship is revealed to the public."

"Makes sense," Commander said, realising in that moment that she had a tight grip on the arm of her chair. "Is the ship supposed to be shaking like this?"

"At first," Samson admitted. "Though, it usually subsides soon enough."

"I may not be an expert on this prototype ship, but it seems as though it is, in fact, getting worse."

Samson paused, looking at his controls as the others went over theirs. It seemed that it *was* out of the ordinary. Something was up, indeed. They struggled to find a solution to what was going on.

"We are off target," the ops officer said finally. "I cannot pinpoint our trajectory."

"How far off target?" Samson demanded.

"It's hard to say," the ops officer replied. "The technology to pinpoint exact positions is not really reliable at these speeds."

"Well, we need to know where we are in relation to other things," Commander added. "Unless we want to fly right through a planet or something."

"I am going over it now," the ops officer explained. "I doublechecked the target point, but it seems to be in a state of flux. I was able to extrapolate from the point we came from and we are very offcourse and locked onto something that I do not believe is the target ship."

"That is impossible!" Samson replied. "We are locked onto a very specific gravitational signature. The way this works, we literally cannot be offcourse."

"Might it be time to stop?" Commander suggested. "Maybe dropping out of slipstream?"

"We can't!" Goran replied. "At these speeds, it's dangerous to manually stop. We need to arrive at a gravitational destination."

"Well, you better find the one you intend to be going to then," Commander replied. "Because if this shaking gets much worse, we are in trouble."

"I don't understand!" Samson replied. "Every target I lock into does not change the course."

"I have a theory," the ops officer spoke up. "There is one thing in this universe that can seemingly double as any gravitational coordinate as it is all and none at the same time."

"A black hole!" Samson exclaimed as he went over the controls. "We seem to be locked to a black hole according to the computer reading it was our target."

"I presume you have not planned for this?" Commander asked.

"We did not think it possible," the ops officer replied. "Any attempt we make now to give a new coordinate might just be another of the black hole's tricks. We might fly right into it."

"Then you have to find some way to find the real coordinate," Commander replied.

"Well, how do we do that?" Samson asked. "I am open to suggestions."

"Honestly, a black hole is literally the most powerful thing out here, right?" Saia commented. "I would imagine that your system is set to lock onto the most powerful signal related to your gravitational target. A ship moving through space would probably be a weaker target."

"Can we reprogram the computer to do that?" Goran asked.

"Of course, we can," the ops officer said as he slid from his seat and pulled a control cover off of a computer bank. "The question is if we have time."

"Well, I believe in you," Commander replied. "And if you cannot, we don't really have time to notice."

The ops officer and another crewman worked away as the ship continued to shake. Samson stayed at the controls, readying himself to input the new coordinates the second they were available. No one wanted to comment about the lack of time; no one wanted to discuss what would happen if they went too close to the black hole. Soon enough, the ops officer gave the go ahead and Goran punched in the controls. For a second, there was nothing but silence.

"We have done it," Samson said in a relieved tone. "We are heading back on course, away from the black hole."

"I am gonna...reprogram the mainframe," the ops officer replied. "To make sure that does not happen again."

The Eyes from the Darkness

The Eyes from the Darkness

The game was much more intense than Mai had expected. She knew it wasn't real, but every fibre of her being was in fight or flight mode—neither of which she could do right then.

"Get away!" Mai shouted, attempting to make her voice as menacing as possible. Her only hope was to scare the wolf off. Perhaps it did not know the trap that she was in. However, as Mai looked into the darkness, two small orbs began to light up with the pale light of the moon. Like tiny mirrors, they reflected the light, but betrayed nothing more than inhuman savage determination. It was the wolf and, worst yet, it seemed to be growing increasingly convinced that an easy meal was at hand.

"Leave me alone!" Mai shouted again. This time the fear showed plainly in her voice. She tried to move, but the more she struggled, the tighter the mud became. She strained to free her hands, the rope dug into her flesh and refused to yield. It felt so real, the pain, the cold—was it *actually* just a game?

The wolf inched forward. It was powerful and fierce, but it was no fool. Humans were sometimes dangerous prey, and in the world of eat and be eaten, it paid to be cautious. A loud, growling bark came from behind Mai. At first, she thought that it was another wolf, but she soon realised it was different. This loud, intimidating barking echoed through the trees and sent chills down Mai's spine. The wolf looked around, before deciding to temporarily retreat. Mai took a small breath of relief as she heard the wolf run off, but worried if the newcomer might be worse. She looked around behind her as best she could with her inability to turn hampering her. A rustle of grass came from beyond the mud and Mai's heart skipped a beat as she waited to see what the new sounds would reveal itself as.

However, it was no wolf or night monster that emerged; instead it was a small red fox with brown tips on its ears and tail. It paused and looked up at Mai with a curious expression on its face.

"Was that you?" Mai asked, not really sure why she was talking to a fox. "You used the echoes to scare it. That was amazing."

The fox bobbed its head, as if it understood her. It seemed to be part of the game. Probably programmed to respond to her. She decided she might as well see what it could do for her.

"Well, you bought me some time," Mai said with a nervous laugh. "Now, I have to figure out how to get out of this."

The fox leapt forward. It's small paws were too light to sink into the mud, she noted, as it ran up to Mai. It carefully climbed up her leg and onto her coat. Then, the fox carefully turned around and began to chew the ropes that bound her hands.

"You are amazing!" Mai said, relieved. She didn't know how the fox knew to do what it was doing, but was nonetheless happy at the turn of events. A howling started up in the darkness. It was fairly far away, but was, Mai was sure, definitely the wolf from before. Any relief Mai felt over the distance was rapidly quelled as another howl responded to the first, then another, and another. The wolf was startled by the fox's deception, but it was calling for help and would soon be back and ready to fight—this time with backup.

The fox gnawed at the ropes, eventually snapping one and causing the rest to loosen. In a matter of moments, she was free. Mai brought her hands in front of her and rubbed her sore, rope-burned wrists. The fox climbed down and looked off in the direction of the howling, seemingly quite concerned, then it looked back to Mai.

"Yeah. I got to get out of here," Mai agreed with a nod, grabbing her legs and pulling. However, even with her hands, she discovered that she could not free her feet. The mud had formed too firm a grip on her thick boots. As the wolves howled again, sounding closer and with an urgent edge, Mai crouched down and began to undo her laces. She fumbled with cold fingers that were still slightly numb from being tightly tied. She managed to undo her laces and began to tug at her feet. Behind her, Mai heard the rustling of brush and *even* more howls in the night—she had to hurry. The mud was tight and it did not want to easily give up her feet. But a few more strong tugs freed one foot, then the other. Mai considered for a second to try to free her boots, but decided it was not worth the risk. She had to move before the wolves surrounded her. The fox looked up at her before heading off. Mai knew her best hope was to follow it. She ran as fast as her legs could carry her. The ground was rough and cold under her stocking feet, but she knew the jaws of the chasing wolves would be far worse. If this was a traditional game, she had beaten the first level—but things would only get harder from there.

What You Can Spare?

What You Can Spare?

I have travelled worlds before, but the alien forest was like nothing I had experienced before. It was like a labyrinth of corridors designed at random that made no sense. Were it not for Athen and her uncanny grasp of navigation, we would have been hopelessly lost. She knew how to read the planet's orange sun and, even with the thick tree cover above, could figure out which way we were going. Yves proved gifted in finding us clear paths through and keeping us out of danger. Things like predatory bugs, massive rodents and deadly quicksand seem to wait just beyond every clearing. I find that many challenges are present in front of you and, as a result, easy to face. This world, with its mysteries and hidden dangers...is something else entirely.

It is easy to lose track of time in such a place. I thought it was still afternoon yesterday and when the sun went down it caught me by surprise. It is literally a different world in here. It makes me wonder how the ancient travellers spent so much time here. Few traverse this place and even the paths—where there still are paths—are long since overgrown from a state of disrepair. Every once and awhile we would find a small patch of concrete from roads of ancient colony times. It is hard to think of the overgrown jungle as having been once a place where people willingly travelled.

The remoteness of the enchanted forest offers us one advantage. The bounty hunters on our heels have been slowed down as well. It is hard to track and follow anyone in the place as it was, but the chaotic way we are zigzagging toward our destination can't be easy for them either. However, the threat is ever-present. I can almost feel their commander's presence... and when the trees sway in the wind...I think he is always about to step out to challenge us. It was easy for me to pretend it was all in my mind, until Ferris came into the clearing and told us to crouch down.

"There is movement," Ferris said, her voice calm and deliberate. "They are over the ridge to the north."

"Are you sure it's them?" I asked, wanting desperately for her to be wrong.

"It is them all right," Ferris responded. "They are luckily on the other side of that ridge. They do not seem to know about the crossing near here so they will have to go around. We have the advantage of not being seen and can move accordingly."

"Alright," I replied with a nod. "Let's keep moving."

The near run-in left us all on edge; we feared every crack, every dancing shadow. We had eluded the mercenaries before, but our luck could not hold out forever. We had to find the ancient colonial archive. If we could get inside with the colonial primer, we would be in the clear.

As we got closer, we began to feel frustrated. According to the map, the way we had been going we should be almost on top of it. However, as much as we looked, as much as we searched, we could not find it. We began to grow frustrated, sure that we had made some sort of mistake, when we found a strange man leaning against a tree. Our first instinct was that he was with the mercenaries. But he seemed to be unarmed, his cloak and clothing patchwork and mixed with moss from the forest.

"Greetings, young ones," the strange man said as he looked up. "It has been some time since I have met anyone here."

"Who are you?" Athen asked, stepping forward as if she were going to try and defend us.

"I am but a merchant," the old man replied. "I am not one to be feared. I know this forest...this world."

I paused, thinking that a man who seemed so proficient at surviving in the forest might know something about its secrets. "Do you know where the ancient colonial archive is?"

"Alan!" Athen snapped. "We don't know if we can trust him."

"Well, we have to trust someone," Ferris pointed out. "We need help if we are to find it before you-know-who finds us."

I looked back at the old man. "Do you know where the archive is?"

"I have been on this world for many years," the old man replied. "There is little that goes on here or is hidden that I do not have knowledge of."

"Then tell us," Athen insisted.

"As with many things in this world, information is not free," the old man replied. "I will hand over the knowledge you seek for some rations."

"We don't have much to spare!" Athen snapped. "We can't waste it here."

"I ask no more than you can spare," the old man replied. "Whatever you offer I will take."

Ferris and Athen looked to me, seeming to want me to confirm that we should trust the strange man. I had no idea how to find the archive, so it seemed like there was everything to be gained by trying and little to be lost other than some coin. "Give him a few rations. We can spare it."

Athen nodded and handed the rations to the man. He did not count it; he did not say anything other than to raise a hand and point to a spot in a clearing beyond. For a second, the three of us looked where he pointed and thought we might have been swindled. However, as we looked, we saw an opening. The archive was overgrown like the paths, and hard to spot with the naked eye unless you knew where to look. We would have searched for days and not found it.

"Thank you!" I said as I looked to the man, but he seemed to have already left.

"This world is full of surprises," Athen said as she looked around.

"I think there is a few more before we are done here," I admitted. "Let's go and hope that the mercenaries have the same issues finding it that we did."

The Safe
Way Across

The Safe Way Across

The fox moved fast through the brush, but seemed to be careful to not move so fast that Mai could not follow. Regardless, Mai pushed herself. She ran as quickly as she could; her heart beating hard from both exertion and fear. Why did the game *seem* so real? Why could her body not tell the difference?

The fox came to a stop at the edge of a river. The deep, fast-moving water raced by in a blur, roaring as it smashed into boulders. The fox jumped to a nearby rock then to one beyond. It looked back as if wanting Mai to follow.

"You want me to come with you?" Mai asked as she gauged the distance between the rocks. "If I fall in that water, it's game over!"

The fox just looked back at Mai, waiting. As the wolves howled again, Mai realised that even if she stayed on the bank, she was done for anyway. She might as well try for the rocks—she might have a chance to survive. Mai took a step back before rushing forward, clumsily jumping to the first rock. Her slick stocking feet slid slightly when she landed. The fox then jumped to another rock, showing her the safest path across. Mai followed, jumping from rock to rock. Each landing tore at her stockings, but the added traction of her bare soles made each one easier— albeit slightly colder. Mai usually was not one to put up with such discomfort. She was the kind of girl that feared ripping or snagging her clothes. Mai's clothes were not even real. This was a game. She found it increasingly harder to remember that the game was not real. Every fibre of her mind desperately screamed that it was real. That her life was in danger. That it was happening right then and there.

The fox finally made the last jump to the opposite bank and Mai hastily followed. She was happy to be back on dry, solid land and looked back. Instantly, she watched black shadows form in the dark.

The wolves rushed to the opposite bank, stopping mere inches from the water. There were seven in all—each formidable and terrifying in its own right. They took turns growling and barking at her as they looked at the raging water and judged their chances. The fox defiantly barked back, almost daring the larger and clumsier wolves to make the attempt.

"Do it!" Mai challenged, realising what the fox was trying to do. "Come and get me!"

The wolves barked and nipped at each other, trying to convince one of their pack to make the attempt. One of the wolves, a pale white one, inched forward, looking at one of the rocks before attempting the jump. He made it onto the first rock, clawing on the slick surface as he tried to keep his balance. However, as he tried the second jump he misjudged the distance, ending up in the water instead. He thrashed and kicked but the current was too strong, sweeping him down and away, smacking against several rocks as he went. The other wolves just looked across at Mai and the fox, looks of anger and frustration plain on their inhuman faces. One of the wolves, a dark grey with a scratched and scared muzzle, moved forward. He locked eyes with Mai, a look of savage hunger and desire clear as the brightness of the moon. It turned and looked up river, running off and leaving his pack to follow. Mai did not have to think long to realise what he was doing.

"He knows a way across," Mai commented. "Somewhere safer."

The fox nodded, indicating Mai to follow it again. Mai eagerly agreed, knowing that if it weren't for the little fox she would have been wolves dinner already. The fox lead Mai deeper and deeper into the forest, still moving quickly but slow enough so Mai was not at a run she could not maintain. Branches and bushed snagged and tore at Mai's coat and dress. She just kept pushing on, leaving bits of fabric and cotton behind as she went.

Better than
the Computer

Better than the Computer

The experimental vessel streaked through the slipstream at a pace faster-than-light toward its destination. With the previous issues behind them, Commander was interested to see the part that came next. With the gravitational coordinates locked, it seemed that the other ship was barely moving as the prototype ship approached it. It all seemed so calm—so easy—it was hard to think that both vessels were hundreds, if not thousands, of tons of metal compressed with heat and oxygen. This was a precise thing and if either ship so much as bumped the other the wrong way it would spell disaster for both crafts.

"Prepare docking approach," Gorman said as he took his hands off the controls.

"Is that not your job on the helm?" Commander asked. "To dock us?"

"Normally, it would be," Samson said as a young woman stepped forward and took her place in front of a series of holocontrols. It lit up, simulating both ships in a real-time relation with each other. Samson looked at the Commander with a proud smile. "Normally a ship approaching a dock is fairly simple. In space with no wind resistance or gravity, it is easy to have automated systems create the approach. However, out here there is more at stake. The computer is manually correcting our parallel slipstream course and any hand beyond the computer that moves it needs to keep that in mind."

"And she can?" Commander asked as she watched the woman guide the simulated holographic ships closer to one another.

Samson nodded. "All of us here are pretty much stock. Helm, engineering, all fairly easy to replace. However, she is something that is much rarer. She has a grasp on special physics that is almost faster than the computer. She is capable of getting a real feel for the motion of the docking. We actually failed every simulation when the computer tried to do it. However, when we found her, we got a hundred per cent success rate."

"A hundred per cent?" Commander asked. "She can beat the machine?"

"The machine is technically faster and more able to sort the data," Samson replied. "However, there is a certain human factor—the gut feeling, the flow of actions that the computer cannot grasp. As she did the simulations, the computer got better, getting more proficient in docking. Eventually, she will teach the computer to do as she does, but until then we need her."

"Makes sense to why you would need her now," Commander commented. "This being the first real practical use of the system."

"We're docked," the docking pilot said as she lowered her hands and the simulations disappeared. "I will be in my quarters if you need me.

Commander looked at the viewscreen and indeed saw the ship docked with the larger vessel. "Just like that eh? She's good."

"You have no idea," Samson replied with a laugh.

Too Close
to Real

Too Close to Real

M ai looked down at her body, still unable to tell if she was digitalised or if it was somehow playing things in her head. She was used to being so different in games, most projecting a powerful male hero or a sexy armoured girl. She was not used to being herself, and this made her feel more vulnerable—however, that was likely the point. She did not know the genre of the game, and it seemed to have horror elements, adventure, puzzles. It seemed as fast as she figured it out, the more it changed.

She looked down at her intelligent fox companion. "So, what do I call you?" Mai asked the fox as they walked. "You are my hero of the night. I can't just call you Fox, can I?"

The fox just looked back as it walked.

"How about Fyre?" Mai offered. "You are red and brave."

The fox looked back again, seemingly happy enough with the name.

"Well, my name is Mai," Mai said in a polite tone as if she would introduce herself to an equally polite stranger. "Am I supposed to tell you who I am in the real world? I am not sure what my in-game backstory is."

Fyre continued to lead on, glancing back every so often to make sure that Mai could still see it. It could, of course, not take part in the conversation, but it looked as if it were listening for no better reason than to keep Mai in good spirits.

"I work in retail in the real world," Mai continued. "Though, gaming is really my thing. I got a popular Let's Play channel...I like to think I am pretty good. Though, I just wish I could remember more of how I got in here."

Fyre looked back, seemingly apologetic. It was choosing the best safe paths through the woods so as to make it easy on Mai. Mai's leggings were long since destroyed, leaving her on uncertain woody terrain in her bare feet. Her coat proved resilient enough, and even with the snares, it was still providing warmth. As long as she stayed in her coat and kept dry, she could compensate for her cold bare feet.

Howls began again from the dark. They were close and getting closer. The wolves had, as she had feared, found a way over the river and their speed was much more than Mai and the fox could manage.

"They are coming for us," Mai replied. "They are a lot smarter and faster than we thought."

Fyre looked around, trying to think of some sort of way to outsmart the wolves as neither it nor Mai could hope to fight them—even though they had taken care of one already. Fyre ended up looking up at the trees, moving its head around and trying to plan an idea. After it looked to Mai to see what she might be able to make of the plan.

"You want us to climb up into the trees?" Mai asked as she looked up, trying to evaluate if she could do such a thing. "As much as I usually am not good with heights, I would be inclined to give it a try. Sure beats the alternative and I would imagine that the wolves aren't just hungry at this point. I think we made them hate us."

Fyre took a moment going from tree to tree. It seemed to know that Mai would not have done something like this before and it would have to lead her as it did with the rocks. As another set of howls echoed into the night, Fyre made its decision as it seemingly found the best tree they were going to find under the circumstances. With its claws, Fyre was easily able to get up the trunk of the tree, stopping on a low hanging branch. Fyre went to the edge, dipping it down low enough for Mai to reach. Mai went up on her toes, grabbing the branch and trying to swing her legs up. She tried to wrap them around it but missed the first couple of times. On the third try she managed to get her feet around the branch, her body dangling below. She spared a look back and was not prepared for what she saw. There were several sets of mirror-like eyes bobbing along, the wolves running toward her at full speed. She had to get up onto the branch, she was a sitting duck if she just hung there.

Mai strained with all her strength, heaving her body up slowly. Just before the wolves arrived, she managed to rotate up and onto the branch. The muzzle of a wolf snapped shut in the spot her leg had been just seconds before. Another few seconds later, and she would have felt teeth in her flesh. Mai slowly stood and stabilized herself on the branch. The wolves began to circle the tree, the bolder ones taking turns trying to climb up.

The First Team

The First Team

On the battleship, Commander headed to the briefing room. Her crew had gathered, and they all seemed ready to find out what was going on. She was not usually one for speeches, so she simply nodded to them before handing out the prepared mission briefings. They all went over the details: the lost planet, the lack of information and a cover-up. Commander sat down and gestured to Kila—the brains behind the details.

Lieutenant stood up in front of the group. "I am sure many of you are wondering how a world that was beginning to be colonised falls like this, and no one knows about it. We are soldiers whose job it is to prevent things like this from happening. There are a lot of theories and conspiracies about the money changing hands—but that is not important. The thing that *is* important is the fact that team Falcon was involved."

"Team Falcon?" Private broke in. "That is amazing!"

"I am not sure I am familiar with team Falcon," Chief admitted.

"Well, we are terraforming exterminators," Commander commented. "We are from a long tradition of soldiers trained for the eradication of dangerous alien species found on new worlds. Back in the early days of terraforming, simple soldiers did it. It turned out to be a challenging enterprise and they started training people like us to do it. Team Falcon was the first team and they were good."

"Until they all retired," Private replied. "Kind of a mystery."

"It really isn't," Lieutenant added. "This is what I was able to uncover with my connections. The first team that was sent had little to no intel about what they had to expect. In the rush of terraforming two planets at the same time, the survey team was occupied in the other world. So, they went in blind. The team went incommunicado almost instantly. They took a survey flight and saw that there was a significant alien presence. Team Falcon was called in and sent to the world. They were sent in force and left on the planet to take care of it. They were so confident that team Falcon had it covered that they went back to work on the other planet. However, the moment they took the focus off the team...they were decimated...only one message getting off the planet."

"What did it say?" Private asked, clearly caught up in the mystery.

Lieutenant paused as if thinking how best to repeat it. "We have found hell."

"That's less than encouraging," Private admitted. "No distress calls, no intel?"

"None," Lieutenant replied. "An extraction ship was sent, but they also lost contact with it. At this time, the corporation had to think of what it could mean. They were stretched really thin, and the very public terraforming failure mixed with the fact they lost a team, they were faced with a conundrum."

"More like a dollar figure," Chief admitted. "They had to think what it would cost them to admit to the failure versus what it would cost to cover it up. It is a common thing and corporations and governments have been doing it for years."

"Well, that is not our concern," Commander said in her deep and authoritative tone. "We work for the company and their best interest. They do not want this blown open. Our plan will be to go to this world and determine if it can be cleared."

"We will see if we can find out what happened to team Falcon," Lieutenant added. "But that is secondary."

"The planet is a prime real estate," Chief commented with a laugh. "Dangerous or not...they want to see if it can make them some money yet."

33

Tree to Tree

Tree to Tree

Mai felt fatigued, her muscles tight—the game was *so* real, and she could not tell her body otherwise. She was used to lives, points, other programs limiting her. She had slain dragons on mountains before with just her wit and a sword. However, in this place, it was her own body that limited her, and it was scary how close they got it. She had to hang on, she had to push herself. Then, there was the fear. She did not fear the dragon, but the wolves below? They terrified her.

"Can wolves climb trees?" Mai asked Fyre as she saw them making progress and nearly reaching high enough to snap at her feet.

Fyre just looked up, seemingly uncertain.

"They seem to be desperate to try," Mai said with a nod. "Can we go higher?"

Fyre went back to its task, climbing and marking out which branches it thought were the easiest and safest. Mai focused on going up and kept her sights high. Not only would the height threaten to cause vertigo, the hungry wolves was not any less of a scary sight. Soon, Mai and Fyre were high up in the trees. The wolves were but shadows below; the ground too far away to see in the diminished light.

"Okay, we need a new plan," Mai admitted as she sat down on a branch to gather her strength. "I don't foresee them giving up any time soon. They have expended so much energy, they aren't leaving until they get something to eat."

Mai looked forward, noticing that at the higher height the trees were rather close together, the branches sometimes overlapped from tree to tree. Fyre seemed to understand what was going on leaping from one tree to another and testing the path. It looked back and encouraged her to follow.

Slowly, tree-by-tree, the pair made their escape. They knew the wolves could not really see them, but they could probably hear them. Moving hastily was dangerous, as the slightest noise could alert the wolves to their plan. Their best hope was that the wolves wouldn't realise they had made a getaway until it was too late.

Mai usually was the kind of girl who liked everything to go as planned and for a few things to change. She usually did not like surprises and was more than happy with the status quo. However now that she was here, climbing from tree to tree she had to admit, despite the fear of being eaten...she was not having a terrible time. Though the game was too real, it was fun, she was finding enjoyment out of it...which was admittedly the point. She seemed to be getting better at the climbing and exploring and this was good if she was to continue to survive in this strange game she had ended up. She looked up at the stars, wondering when morning would finally come.

"Do you think the wolves will give up when the sun comes up?" Mai whispered...wondering again why she was talking to a fox.

Fyre shot back a look that seemed none to encouraged of the possibility of the wolves simply abandoning the hunt. Mai wondered what it was about her that was driving them so mad. Was there something about her that they found irresistible or were they just incredibly hungry. Either way, as long as she had options and she had strength, she would continue her fight for survival. She was glad to have Fyre and thankful was still eager to help.

Soon the close-packed trees came to an end. A rocky hills cape rested before them and the sparse trees would no longer allow

for horizontal climbing. They would have to climb down and
make their way up into the hills by foot.

"Do you think they are still at the first tree?" Mai asked. "And if
so are we far enough away?"

Fyre looked back the way they had come before looking back
with an unsure look on its small animal face.

"I guess we have to risk it," Mai agreed, slowly and carefully
beginning the descent down. As the ground came into closer view,
she paused. Where were the wolves? She knew that they were
cunning. Mai would not put it past them to be lurking in the dark,
waiting for her to come to them. However, she knew they could not
stay in the trees forever and had to get to higher ground. Mai
lowered herself down, her feet crushing softly into the foliage
below. She reached up and helped Fyre down, looking around in
silence before moving away slowly toward the rocky hillside.

Fyre jumped from Mai's arms and began to look up at the
hillside, considering their options.

In Your Body
or in Your Head

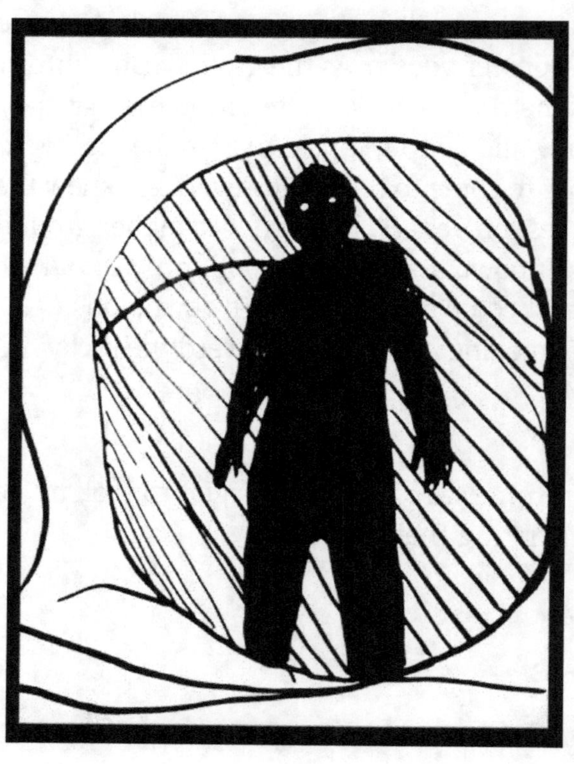

In Your Body or in Your Head

Mai felt hungry and this raised a whole myriad of questions about the game. Was the game simulating her hunger like it simulated her body and cold, or was her body hungry in the real world? Could she eat something here and be satiated, or would it persist until she had something real? Those questions only made her more confused, and she tried to focus on the task at hand.

"Do you know of any way through there? Maybe we can lose them."

Fyre nodded, heading off and Mai followed. As they climbed the slopes, the howls of the wolves were heard again. They sounded like they were still back at the original tree, but must have figured out that Mai and Fyre were no longer there. They would start to look for them again. Eventually, they would find the hill and try to get them here. Mai hastened her step, moving as fast as her feet would carry her safely over the rocky, sloped terrain. Soon, the pair reached a large cave mouth, leading deep into the mountain. A pale light could be seen from the other side...there was a path that led right through. However, Fyre stopped, sniffing something and looking very concerned. Mai felt something in the stone by one of her feet. She crouched and found a long massive claw mark on the ground.

"Is that from a bear?" Mai asked in a concerned tone. "Is this tunnel a bear's den?"

Fyre just looked up with fear in its eyes. Wolves howled in the distance. Mai leaned out and could see several small shadows moving toward where they had started up the mountain. It would take only moments for the wolves to catch up with them.

"I think we should try to make our way through," Mai said with a nod. "With luck, the bear is sleeping."

Fyre looked at the cave again, clearly not very keen on the idea. However, when it looked back toward the direction of the wolves, it did not like that much more either.

"It will be alright," Mai said as she picked Fyre up. "The advantage with the bear is it is not after us—yet. And with any luck, we can keep it that way."

Mai inched along, careful to walk softly and make as little noise as she could. She could barely see in the low light of the cave, but it appeared Fyre could see just fine. When the small fox wanted her to go forward, it would Mai's arm forward. To stop, it pushed down, and to either side the direction she could go. This went on for several minutes—the dark surrounding Mai and the light seeming so far off in the distance. A strange warmth was felt ahead and a rumbling that started slow. However, the sound grew to a deep baritone then back again. It was the snore of a massive figure—it was the bear!

Mai struggled not to gasp, to keep herself as quiet as possible. She could not see the enormous beast, but she knew that it was there. She shuffled slowly, almost cursing her heart for the sound of its beats. Soon, she was past it and breathed a silent sigh of relief as the snoring went on uninterrupted. Mai fought the urge to run, knowing that the smacking of running feet might wake it up. As she made it a few more steps, she realised the cave had grown silent. She waited for more snoring, but none came. The bear was awake, and she could hear the sounds of it getting up.

Mai held her breath and froze in place. She glanced over her shoulder and saw the silhouette of the massive creature against the night back the way they came. However, when the bear moved, it did not move toward her, instead toward the other end of the cave where a pair of small figures were silhouetted against the sky. It was the wolves! The wolves woke up the bear, and it wasn't happy with that.

As the sounds of wolves fighting bear erupted, Mai decided that it was time to run. She sprinted as fast as her legs would carry her to the opposite end of the tunnel. The other end was smaller, first making her crouch and then crawl. By the time she and Fyre were out again into the night air, the hole was barely large enough to allow Mai through. She allowed one last look back, hearing the whimpering of wolves and deciding that they were very unlikely to try and follow her—at least through the way the pair come through.

The Cycle Renewed

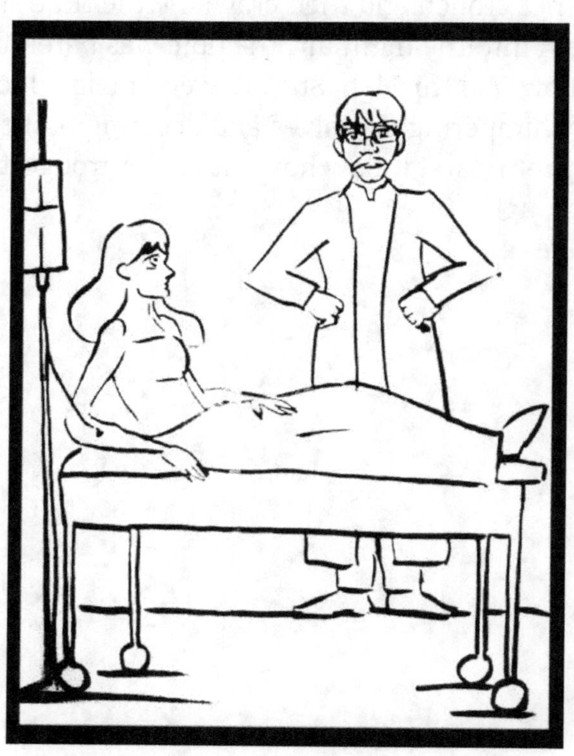

The Cycle Renewed

Once on the other end of the clearing, Fyre continued to lead Mai. It had grown more eager and seemed like they were close to where she was taking her. Soon, they ended up in a strange ruin, the remnants of stone walls dotted the area from a long-gone, ancient structure. Mai looked around curiously.

"What is this place?" she asked as she walked on.

Fyre lead Mai deep inside and to a large glowing stone in the centre. Mai was mystified, watching her reflection on the enigmatic stone. Fyre walked up to the bottom and put a paw up against it. Then, it looked up like it wanted Mai to do the same. Mai nodded, having trusted the fox so far she might as well. She put her hand to the stone but gasped as it stuck like glue instantly. She tried tugging it free, but her hand was now fused to the magic stone. Mai looked over to Fyre and was shocked to discover that instead of the reflection of a fox cast on the stone was the reflection of a tall girl with red hair. The reflection looked toward Mai.

"I am sorry," the girl in the reflection said in a sombre tone. "This is how the game is played and I have to win."

"You are a player, too?" Mai asked, confused, as she continued to tug at her hand. She could feel a numbing feeling going up her forearm and toward her elbow. She began to feel weak and sleepy.

"This is the only way," the girl replied. "I rescued you so you could take my place. You must do the same. Someday, someone will find a way to break the cycle, but until then there must always be a fox and a girl."

"Please, no," Mai pleaded as she felt the numbness take over, seeing spots in her eyes and having issues remaining conscious. "We...came so...far."

"Do not worry," the girl responded. "They will send someone to you, soon."

Darkness filled Mai's vision and reality fell away. As consciousness began to come back, she felt like there was something wrong. She was back in the forest, the night seemingly refreshed and new above her. As she rolled to get up, something felt different. She was smaller and furrier. She struggled to her feet, finding out she was on four paws. She looked down at one and saw orangey-brown fur. She tried to speak but found she could only mew and bark. She was now a fox—like Fyre. Mai looked around, swirling in place and getting used to her new form. Fyre was nowhere to be seen, fox form or otherwise. Was this really how the game was played? How was the cycle started? Mai fought for answers, but found none. Her concentration was broken by a sound in the distance.

"Hello?" an unfamiliar feminine voice called out. "Is this some kind of game? Is anyone there? I'm lost and tied. I need help, please!"

Mai looked on in horror, realising yet another girl had been stranded in the game. She knew there were dangers and predators afoot and the only way she could be human again was to help her—to trick her. Mai headed off in the direction of the girl...

And the cycle began again.

Meanwhile, back in a lab, a scientist stood over a young girl with red hair. She sat up slowly, groggy and confused. The scientist pulled a device off her head and smiled. "Rest, girl. You have won the game. For you, this is over. But for others...it has just begun."

About The Author

R alph K Jones is an Australian author and storyteller whose works serve as a contemporary response to primeval human truths. His inspiration comes from real-life experiences, ancient tales and daily ethical dilemmas, which he rewrites and transforms into futuristic Sci-fi and dystopian stories. While the stories have clear messages, Ralph is determined not to tell his readers what to think. His writing took off after the birth of his first child when he would write down the stories he told her at night, so in future, his other children could enjoy the same tales in the future 600 stories later, and his children are now growing up fast it's time to share these adventures with the world.

A firm believer in individuality, he hopes that he can encourage people to think for themselves—going against the herd and doing what is right, not merely what's expected. His writing demonstrates an adoration and respect for the human experience, which Ralph believes has remained fundamentally unchanged at its core. Through stories, let there be no doubt people can share lessons and help each other. You can visit him online at www.ralphkjones.com or on Twitter (@RalphKJones).

Continue Your Journey

Further must read collections from Ralph K Jones include:

ETHICAL DISPLACEMENT

GRAVITATIONAL MOMENTUM

QUANTUM DILEMMAS

GENETIC INHERITANCE VOLUMES ONE TO TWO

THORIUM HALF LIFE VOLUMES ONE TO FOUR

ANTHROPIC PRINCIPLES VOLUMES ONE TO SIX

QUANTUM ATTRACTION VOLUMES ONE TO SIX

QUANTUM AWAKENING VOLUMES ONE TO TWELVE

QUANTUM ENTANGLEMENT VOLUMES ONE TO TWENTY-ONE

9 798653 834776